A NEW MOTHER FOR THE TWINS

MAIL ORDER BRIDES OF MISSOURI

SUSANNAH CALLOWAY

Tica House Publishing

Sweet Romance that Delights and Enchants!

PERSONAL WORD FROM THE AUTHOR

Dearest Readers,

Thank you so much for choosing one of my books. I am proud to be a part of the team of writers at Tica House Publishing who work joyfully to bring you stories of hope, faith, courage, and love. Your kind words and loving readership are deeply appreciated.

I would like to personally invite you to sign up for updates and to become part of our **Exclusive Reader Club**—it's completely Free to join! We'd love to welcome you!

Much love,

Susannah Calloway

VISIT HERE to Join our Reader's Club and to Receive Tica House Updates!

https://wesrom.subscribemenow.com/

CONTENTS

CHAPTER 1

When Bailey Evans looked back on that day years later, he would wonder why nothing had seemed amiss as he went about his work at the Hardware and Tinware Shop that spring afternoon. He had never imagined tragedy striking suddenly and without warning; he had always assumed that when it came, it would be heralded by a storm and thunder.

This assumption proved to be wrong, of course; but he couldn't have known that then.

If he had been paying attention, there had been warning signs, though. Bandits had lately been seen in Rough Creek, the Missouri town where he lived with his mother and his young niece. There were reports that they had been robbing coaches and supply wagons on their way into town, wearing masks with intricate, snake-like patterns to hide their faces, terrifying women in hold-ups.

Only the week before, they had robbed the local bank but had dispersed and fled before the sheriff arrived. No one was able to say who they were or where they were headquartered, which made them even more frightening. It was as though they came crawling out of the prairie grass and retreated back into it once they had finished thieving and shooting and spreading terror. The good people of Rough Creek viewed them as almost a natural occurrence, like the annual plague of locusts or a winter snowstorm. In that light, there was precious little they could do except arm themselves and pray.

As Bailey had been leaving the house that morning on his way to the Hardware and Tinware Shop where he worked six days a week, his niece Elizabeth had emerged onto the front porch. A sharp-eyed girl of fifteen with long auburn hair that fell in waves across her shoulders, she had been living with Bailey and his mother ever since his sister, Naomi, had died of cholera some years before. On most days, she seemed indifferent to his comings and goings, but this morning, unexpectedly, she had hugged him close and said, "Do be careful. I wouldn't want anything terrible to happen to you."

Perplexed by the urgency of the warning, Bailey had laughed. "Careful?" he said. "What sort of terrible things are you expecting to happen to me?"

"There have been some truly bad men doing bad things, lately," Elizabeth said with wide, solemn eyes. "I just worry about you, is all."

"Listen, nothing is going to happen to me," said Bailey. "I'm smart. I know how to stay out of trouble."

"I know, but trouble also has a way of finding you, don't it?" Elizabeth brushed her hair back. She was still wearing her long white flannel nightgown with the lace collar, the one she always wore to bed. She looked pale and ghostly in the tranquil light of mid-morning. "You're one of those men things happen to."

Bailey had never thought about it in those terms, but he supposed she was right. Only the year before, he had been drafted by the sheriff to assist in killing a large bear that had found its way into town and holed up inside the Presbyterian church, having killed several animals and mauled an older gentleman until he bled to death. It was Bailey who had found the creature crouched at the front of the church near the piano in a shaft of fall sunlight; it was Bailey who fired the single shot that ended its life.

After that, for a few weeks he had been something of a town hero. Young, single women had shown up at his door with baskets of fruit and flowers. His mother had asked him why he hadn't shown interest in courting any of them. In truth, Bailey kept asking himself the same question. He didn't have a good answer. But he had courted a woman before and found the experience disappointing. He wasn't sure he wanted to put himself through that again.

"You shouldn't discount yourself," his mother had said, "not when you're still so young."

But Bailey had not listened. He enjoyed the work he did at the Hardware and Tinware Shop. He had some writings—the beginnings of a novel, tucked away inside a desk drawer in their home. His writings were good enough, he thought, that he might be able to launch a career as a novelist someday. He didn't have time to think about getting married. He liked the life he had and didn't want it disrupted.

When he reached the Hardware and Tinware Shop that morning, he found it empty but for Jacob Ashby, his friend and partner, who was standing behind the counter wiping it down with a damp cloth. Jacob gave a low grunt of acknowledgment as he walked in.

"Did you see the fire last night?" he asked. "Young schoolteacher was found passed out from the smoke on the floor of her sitting room. They only just managed to drag her out before the house collapsed."

"No, this is the first I'm hearing about it," said Bailey. "We played Knucklebones and Fox and Geese with Elizabeth and then retired early."

"This would have been about eleven o'clock." Jacob raked a hand through his head of thick curly hair. "It was all the twins could talk about last night. I had a devil of a time getting them to settle down."

Jacob had been raising his twin children, Ethan and Emily, single-handedly ever since the sudden death of his beloved wife five years before. She had survived the childbirth but immediately developed a sickness that killed her within days. Jacob spent the following months in a cloud of grief, trying to manage raising two infants while also running the town's only Hardware and Tinware Shop full-time.

In this, Bailey and his family had proven an unexpected ally: Faye, Bailey's mother, and Elizabeth had agreed to watch the children whenever both Jacob and Bailey were working. It wasn't unusual for Bailey to return home and find them playing a game of romps in the sitting room. Over time, they had come to seem like members of the family. Jacob was more like a brother to them than a friend. He had made no secret of wanting to get married again.

"I was able to get a decent look at the teacher," he told Bailey. "Beautiful lady. Couldn't have been older than twenty. Would have been a real shame if anything had happened to her. Imagine, a whole life cut short like that so suddenly."

Bailey wanted to ask if a young woman could really die like that—it seemed a grave injustice, a transgression of the moral order of the universe—but he knew that it happened. He also knew that Jacob was only too aware that such things happened.

"You ought to have been the one to have saved her," he said aloud. "She'd have fallen in love with you."

"Didn't get there fast enough," said Jacob. "Tobias Garland got there before I did. Imagine his stupid face being the first thing she sees when she comes to. She'll probably marry the danged fool."

"Well, at least she's alive, anyway."

Jacob didn't respond. He was fingering the long-stemmed pipe in his pocket as if contemplating heading outside for a smoke before the inevitable midday influx of customers.

"By the way," he said, "our only shovel went missing last night. Either I misplaced it, or somebody stole it, but I'll need you to run down to the general store and pick up another one." He shoved a wad of money across the counter. "Shouldn't cost you any more than this. Say hello to Rachel for me."

CHAPTER 2

Rachel Deakins was the beautiful single assistant who manned the general store four mornings a week. Jacob was forever contriving reasons for Bailey to go over there. Bailey had never been able to tell whether Jacob was trying to pair them off or if Jacob liked her himself and was simply too shy to make the trips on his own. Jacob wasn't afraid of most things, but more than once, Bailey had seen him flustered into incoherence by an unusually beautiful customer. He had given him no end of teasing a few weeks before when Jacob had been cowed into respectful silence by Reverend Thurgood's flaxen-haired widow.

Jacob followed Bailey outside, drawing his pipe out and lighting it. The sky was graying and the earthy smell of the air presaged rain. "Try not to get into any trouble while I'm gone," said Bailey.

"I'm running away with a lady and leaving you in charge of the store," Jacob said with a smirk.

Half a block down the street, Bailey found Rachel quietly minding the counter in a grey-blue cotton dress with a white collar. Her eyes shone like lamps as he entered the store, inhaling the heady scent of apples and kerosene and salted mackerels. Oranges were stacked in a pyramid atop a pair of barrels at the back of the room. Reaching for a handful of hard candies, he accidentally jostled one of the pyramids with his elbow and oranges went tumbling to the floor, rolling in all directions.

Right away Rachel came running out from behind the counter.

"I'm so sorry," he said. "If I had known I was just going to create more work for you—"

"Here, I've got it," said Rachel, not unkindly, as she knelt and began gathering up the stray oranges. The scent of rosewater on her dress was subtle but potent; Bailey could see why Jacob was smitten with her. "I probably shouldn't have stacked them like that; you're the third customer this morning to knock them over."

Bailey didn't respond. He was only just remembering a dream Elizabeth had experienced the night before, a dream that had left her shaking and terrified at three in the morning. A dream of death and violence…

"Was this all you wanted?" asked Rachel, scooping the candies up and carrying them over to the counter—but at that moment the stillness of the morning was shattered by a series of loud, rapid shots.

Bailey and Rachel exchanged panicked glances. He ran to the door and looked out. In the street, chaos had erupted, with frightened townsfolk running and screaming and crouching behind water troughs amid clouds of dust.

"Bailey, what's going on out there?" Rachel wanted to know. She had to stand on her toes to see over his shoulder. "Who's doing the shooting?"

"I don't know yet," said Bailey. Turning and taking her by the shoulders, he said sternly, "Listen, I don't want you setting foot outside of this building. Not until you know for sure that it's safe. You hear?"

Rachel nodded, clearly frightened by the urgency in his tone. "Bailey, be careful," she said. "Facing a bear is one thing—bears don't carry guns…"

"Don't you worry about me," said Bailey, and without another word, he left the store and ran up the street, in the direction of the noise. A black horse with no rider ran past him at a steady gallop, followed by a herd of half a dozen feral hogs looking badly startled by the sudden commotion.

Perhaps it was just his imagination, but the gunfire seemed to have come from the direction of the Hardware and

Tinware Shop. He had only left a few minutes before, and it was inconceivable to him that thieves could have descended on it so quickly—but then, they had been known to appear like a summer storm. He knew how Jacob would react if the store was robbed during business hours because they had often talked about it; he would grab the gun that was hidden under the counter and fire in their general direction, hoping that they would scatter before he was forced to kill.

"I don't want to kill another living soul," he had said, "but I'll do it if I have to."

But Bailey knew Jacob better than this. "If push came to shove," he had said, "I don't know if you could bring yourself to pull the trigger. They'd sense your hesitation, and they'd flay you alive."

In spite of his bluster, Bailey worried that Jacob was too gentle to survive a robbery. Worse, he would frighten the bandits just enough that they would think nothing of killing him just to save their own hides.

He was just passing the milliner's about twenty yards from the store when a terrible thing happened. Bailey's heart leapt into his throat as the door of the Hardware and Tinware Shop swung open and three men emerged, each of them armed, their faces hidden behind red strips of cloth that looked as though they had been torn from a discarded shirt. Ducking behind a post, Bailey watched as the men mounted horses and rode off, up the street and around the block, firing into the air as they went. Each gunshot provoked dismayed screams from the women and children seeking shelter.

Bailey waited a minute or two just to make sure they weren't coming back, then rose and continued on his way up the street into the Hardware and Tinware Shop. Nothing could have prepared him for what he witnessed as he stepped through the door.

He had left the store only minutes before, but during his brief absence, it had been rendered virtually unrecognizable. The bandits had left the store in complete disarray. Shelves had been overturned and piles of wrenches and hammers now lay scattered across the floor. Bailey had to be careful not to step on any of the seemingly hundreds of loose nails that were now strewn in his path. The long-stemmed pipe that Jacob had been smoking as Bailey left had been split down the middle and lay beneath a stool in a column of dusty sunlight.

Hearing a painful coughing coming from behind the counter, Bailey breathed an urgent silent prayer as he rounded the corner, conscious of his every heartbeat.

There in a pool of blood lay Jacob, still alive, but only just. Blood soaked the front of his vest and shirt where he had been shot in the lungs. His breathing was raspy and seemed to be slowing, like a machine or a clock that had wound down. He made a game attempt at a smile as Bailey knelt down beside him and reached for his hand. The gun that normally lay hidden beneath the counter was resting just a few feet away.

Jacob shook his head, sensing Bailey's unspoken question. "Guess I owe you," he said and then coughed. "You were right. I couldn't bring myself to fire it."

"You don't owe me nothin'," said Bailey. He didn't want to think about what he was seeing in front of him. Maybe if he didn't think about it, it wouldn't prove true. "You're going to be all right," he said. "You're alive. You're breathing."

"Don't lie to yourself, Bailey." The smile faded and a look of pity emerged from behind Jacob's eyes. Pity not for himself but for Bailey. "Don't go feeling sorry for me, now. You're the one who's still got to live in this world after I'm gone. My own troubles are … over."

"Jacob, no." Bailey's tone was frantic. "Don't go talking like this now. I'm sending for a doctor. We're gonna get that bullet out of you. When… when you're better… we'll have ourselves a real celebration. Cakes and jams and hard candies. Anything you want."

Jacob gazed up into his friend's face. "Will there be whiskey?"

"All the whiskey you could ask for."

"And women?"

"Loads of women," said Bailey. "Rachel, the reverend's widow, the schoolteacher… all of 'em saying how brave you were, and how they're proud of you."

Jacob smiled. "Bailey?" he said. "P-promise me one thing."

"Promise." Bailey would have agreed to anything in that moment.

Gripping his hand, Jacob said, "Promise me that after I'm g-gone—you understand? Do you follow me?—promise that you'll take care of the twins for me. Make sure they're fed and clothed and properly educated. A new mother… C-can you do that?"

Bailey nodded, his vision obscured by tears. "Yes, but you're not goin' anywhere, it was just a scuffle, you're just wounded, you'll see 'em this evening—"

But Jacob didn't respond. He had gone completely still, leaving Bailey alone in the suddenly airless room. Wholly insensible of his surroundings, he rested his head against the dead man's chest and wept.

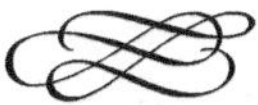

CHAPTER 3

"I've already told you, sweetheart, he's not coming back," said Faye Evans. "He's in heaven. He's passed on."

It had been several days since the funeral, and she, Bailey, and Elizabeth were seated at the kitchen table with Ethan and Emily. The women had prepared a lavish meal of potatoes, sausage, cornbread, corn on the cob and hash. Elizabeth had spent much of the day making a red velvet molasses cake that she planned to serve once the table had been cleared.

The Evans family had never gone hungry in the years since Bailey had taken the job at the Hardware and Tinware Shop. They ate better than most families in Rough Creek. On any other night, Bailey would have been grateful, but tonight he stared listlessly at his plate, having lost all appetite. He kept picturing the ever-expanding pool of blood as Jacob expired on the floor of the store like an animal in a slaughterhouse. Bailey had had no choice but to go in to work on the following day, and whenever he glanced down at the spot—which would never be fully clean—it was like having to relive the experience over again.

"Where's heaven?" asked Ethan, the fair-haired boy of five.

Faye hesitated, looking temporarily stumped by the question. "It's where your mother lives," she said slowly. "Your pa has gone to be with her."

"Please can we go there, too?" asked Emily. "I want to see them."

"No, you can't go there," said Faye, throwing a helpless look at her granddaughter. "Hopefully not for a long time."

"Can we get there by train? Our friend Heloise once tooked a train to Boston. Heaven can't be no further than Boston."

"Heaven is a lot further away than Boston."

Emily's eyes widened at the thought. "Is it on an island in the middle of the sea?"

"Could you swim there?" asked Ethan. "Or would fish eat you?"

"No one gets into heaven until they die," said Faye. "You can go looking for it, but you would never find it. You could search the whole world and the skies and never find it."

This idea seemed to perplex the two children. Faye turned to her son. "Help me out here, Bailey. The children want to know why they can't see their pa."

Momentarily shaken out of his reverie, Bailey said, "The two of you are going to be living with us now." *At least until we find you a new place*, he thought. He wondered if pairing them with a new family would be consistent with the promise he had made to Jacob. Perhaps that was what Jacob had meant when he said to find them a new mother. But until then, they would be staying here.

"When are we going home again?" asked Ethan with all the bluntness of a five-year-old boy. "I'm tired of staying here. I want to be in my own bed."

"Cake's ready," said Elizabeth sweetly, heedless of any tension. "Who wants some?"

Both of the children raised their hands.

"All right, but you're not getting any until you promise to stop pestering us with questions," said Faye as she rose to gather up the plates. "There's only so many times I can answer the same question. You're not getting a different answer the twelfth time."

"They don't understand, Grandma," said Elizabeth, taking the plates from Faye. "They're very young. All they know is their parents are together someplace where they can't go. I'd be confused, too."

"I understand that," said Faye, "but that's no reason to keep asking me things when I've already given my answers. I can't explain heaven any better than I already have."

"This morning I stepped on a grasshopper," said Ethan brightly. "Will it be in heaven?"

"No, bugs don't go to heaven," Faye replied. "Only people and maybe some animals."

"How big is it?" asked Emily.

"I don't know, I've never been there."

"Then how do you know about it?"

"That's enough questions," Faye said impatiently. "I told you that you're not getting any cake until you calm down, and I meant it." Turning to Bailey, she added, "Are you just going to sit there, or would you care to help us?"

"What do you need?" asked Bailey, wanting to be helpful.

"The children need to start getting settled down, if you wouldn't mind."

Bailey, who had precious little experience with small children, had to think quickly. "We're going to play a game," he said, "where we see who can go the longest without saying a single word. Who's ready to play?"

"Ethan is going to lose," said Emily. "He always talks first."

"I do not!" cried Ethan, indignant.

"Yes, you start laughing at me even though I haven't done nothing. And then I laugh, and you say that counts as talking, even though you laughed first."

"All right, all right, we're not going to argue about it," interjected Bailey. "I want everyone to be still and quiet. Concentrate on not saying anything." The kids bristled, silent but restless. "That's it. You're doing a great job. Now keep it up."

"Grandma, would you mind washing the rest of these while I set the plates out?" said Elizabeth quietly—but not quietly enough, as it turned out, for both of the children turned and pointed accusing fingers at her.

"SHE LOSES!" they shouted in chorus.

"I wasn't playing," Elizabeth cried. "Just for that, I don't know if you deserve any cake."

The children made pleading faces, batting their long lashes in a manner that would have melted even the stoniest heart.

"I don't know. Bailey," she said, "what do you think? Have the children been good enough to earn cake?"

"Jacob would let us have it," said Ethan. "He always let us have cake, whether we were good or not."

"He's your father, dear," said Faye in exasperation. "And don't call him Jacob; it's disrespectful."

"You call him Jacob," Ethan pointed out.

"Yes, but he's not my pa. I call him by his name because, well, that's his name."

"He's not my pa, neither," said Ethan with perfect matter-of-factness. "Not anymore. He's dead."

After the cake had been eaten, Bailey went out onto the front porch. It was a clear, cloudless night, and the stars shone in the velvety blackness like jewels on a gloved hand. He lit his pipe and sat for a few minutes in silence, realizing he didn't have any satisfactory answers to the questions the children had been asking. The night was so close, he almost felt Jacob could have stepped down out of it—if he was really up there.

Possibly the strangest quality of loss was the awful hole it seemed to open up in the world. Where once there had been a person, there was now nothing. Bailey knew better than to think Jacob had been synonymous with his body. Jacob was no longer here. Bailey didn't know where he had gone, but he sensed with conviction that he would never find him again in this world.

The door opened, and Faye stepped out onto the porch. "The twins are in bed," she said. "Not to say that they've calmed down. Ethan wants to know if there will be fish in heaven."

"Will there be?" Bailey replied.

Faye sat down in the chair beside him, smoothing the folds of her gingham gown. "I think in some ways, this has been harder for you than it's been for them, hasn't it? They're still too young to really get it. They'll be all right with time. For you, though—well, it must have been a terrible shock."

"It could have been worse." Bailey drummed on the edge of the chair, thinking, his fingers restless. "I s'pose I could have been in the store when it happened. I had only just stepped out. They'd likely have shot both of us."

"I have been thinking about that every day since it happened." Faye's eyes gleamed owl-like in the light from the kerosene lamp. "It must have been some special providence that kept you from being in the store when those bandits descended."

"I don't know if it was providence or just a timely coincidence," said Bailey. He didn't know much of anything lately. It seemed horribly unfair that he should be elected to live when Jacob had died in such a brutal fashion. Bailey hadn't left behind any children. If one of them had to go, he would have been the more sensible choice.

"Darling, I know you don't understand it now," said Faye, "but one day you'll be able to look back and see the past few days with a clearer perspective. We can't always know why things happen when they first happen. Sometimes, it takes some distance to see the hidden purpose behind it."

"Is there a hidden purpose? There sure ain't one that I can see," said Bailey. He kept thinking of Jacob wheezing his last painful breaths and wondering why he couldn't have died in his place. "I can't imagine what sort of providence would take a father away from his two young children."

"I'm not pretending it makes sense to me, either," said Faye. "But like you, I only have part of the picture. I think in time you may come to feel differently. I know how much you miss him. How much your heart aches for what happened to him."

Bailey nodded. "When Nellie broke things off, I didn't think I could ever recover from that. But this is so much worse. It makes the end of that relationship seem like a mild headache. All that time I spent grieving over her. Acting like it was the end of the world. What a waste."

Faye took his hand in hers and patted it. "You weren't wrong to feel upset about it just because something worse has happened. Hearts were only made to hold so much grief."

"Then why does it feel like it never stops coming?"

Faye didn't have a good answer for this. Instead, she went on stroking his hand gently with one thumb like she used to do when he was a boy.

Bailey bore her affection patiently, sensing it would be ungracious to turn her away, even though he felt restless and fidgety. He thought back to the moment he and Jacob had walked out of the store together, Bailey thinking he would be back in a few minutes, and they would carry on their day as before. He tried to remember what he said to him as they were walking out the door. He couldn't remember now—that was how trivial it had been. He ought to have hugged his friend, but these things never occurred to a person in the moment. He had no way of knowing then that they were walking together for the last time.

"Emily said something very strange just as I was putting her down," said Faye. "I told her that before she shut her eyes, I wanted her to pray for her ma and pa in heaven. And she looked up at me with those big blue eyes of hers and said, 'When is my new mommy coming?'"

Bailey was stunned. He hadn't realized the full extent of the trauma the two children must be suffering until this moment. "That poor soul. What did you say to her?"

"I mean, what does one say to that?" Faye replied. "I told her if she prayed hard enough, maybe she would get a new mommy. And you want to know something? I don't think that was wrong, exactly. At least, I think it's good for children to pray for things like that."

"Yes, but don't go giving her false hope," said Bailey in a warning tone.

"I didn't make any promises," said Faye. "I said maybe. I told her to pray about it, and we would see. I don't want her waiting at the window for a lady to appear." Faye fell silent, and when she spoke again, it was in a lowered voice. "That girl needs a ma, though. Me and Rebecca can't raise them by ourselves, as much as we love them. Not forever, anyway. I'm getting on in years, and Rebecca will be leaving once she finds a man of her own. For them kids to lose both of their parents before the age of six—it's just unthinkable."

Unthinkable, yes, Bailey wanted to say. And yet it happened all too often. Especially out here in lawless places like Rough Creek.

Faye squeezed his hand once, lovingly, then rose and went inside. Bailey sat stroking the stem of his pipe, thinking. If things hadn't ended so badly with Nellie, they could have been a mother and father to the children. Somehow, he didn't think Jacob would have minded that. But of course, there would be no convincing Nellie to revive the relationship, and anyway, he wasn't sure he could have married her after the grief she had put him through. When she walked away, she had made it clear she didn't want him contacting her again. Somehow that was the worst part of it, the finality of loss, the knowing that there was no repairing what was broken.

But at least Nellie was still living. As Ethan had so bluntly put it at dinner, Jacob was dead. No medicine in the world could bring him back.

CHAPTER 4

"Of course, this won't be the last time you see us, dear," said Aunt Ruth. "You'll come back and visit, or we'll come and see you. We're a family. We love each other too much to spend the rest of our lives separated."

"Don't make promises you can't keep," said Kathryn Sandridge, a woman of twenty-two, with long blonde hair framing a slender, pale face. She and her aunt and cousins were standing on the platform of a train station in Boston. Kathryn was preparing to board the train for a new home out west. "You mightn't have the money to see me, or I mightn't have the money to see you."

"Kate, you mustn't say such things," said her cousin Natasha, holding a nankeen handkerchief in front of her face. "Do you remember when I was lost in the Alleghenies with a snowstorm barreling in, and how James came and found me? Family always finds a way."

"I wish that were true," said Kathryn, who prided herself on her unsentimental view of the world. "I'm grateful that he found you, though, or you wouldn't be standing here now to say goodbye to me. I'll probably be forgotten by the time the train pulls out of the station—"

"You won't!" said Natasha, stomping her foot.

"But if ever you happen to think of your old cousin," Kathryn said with a wry smile, "remember to send me a letter and let me know how the family's doing."

"And you, as well," said Aunt Ruth. "We'll be wanting to know if you're eating enough, and if you've been kidnapped, and whether your husband is hiding the bodies of his other wives in a closet."

"Let's pray that he isn't," said Kathryn, laughing. "Based on the letters he's sent me, he sounds like a real gentleman. His spelling is a little—well, *creative*—but he works hard. I imagine he is too busy."

"Love, they're all going to say that." Ruth gave her a small kiss on the forehead. "They won't want you to be getting jealous. If you should find out that he's already courted a lady, I hope you'll keep that in mind. There will be surprises. There always are. Not all of them will be pleasant."

"I'm afraid there won't be many surprises from my side, anyway," said Kathryn. "I'm just who I seem to be. I haven't got anything to hide."

"No, and we love you for it." Ruth gazed deeply into her eyes. Kathryn could almost read the question that was forming there. "Does he know about—"

"I might have mentioned it," said Kathryn quietly. "He told me he wasn't bothered by it. He says stranger-looking people than me come into his store every day." She laughed. "He says he might be one of them."

Aunt Ruth smiled a benevolent smile. "Well, if he doesn't mind that, then he's perfect for you."

Kathryn didn't respond. She was conscious of a man walking slowly past, eyeing her disdainfully. People never bothered to hide their stares, not when a person looked like she did. Kathryn had been born with eyes of two different colors, one brown and the other blue. All her life she had struggled to make friends because of her uncanny appearance. Once she had been disinvited from a dinner party when the host got a good look at her. Another time she had been discreetly asked to leave a church because she was inadvertently stirring up fear in the hearts of the congregation—they felt she must have been sent by the devil and were praying that she would repent. When Aunt Ruth had heard this news, she had marched down to the church and given a speech that the parishioners still spoke of in whispers.

"Maybe you'll find better company there," said Natasha. "I'm sorry the people here weren't always as accepting as they should have been. You are the best person I know. When they called you a child of the devil, they were just exposing their own ignorance."

It was the most emphatic declaration of solidarity that Natasha had ever given her, and Kathryn's appreciation was plain on her face.

"It's been a joy growing up with you," she said. "I'm sorry it happened the way it did—but I sometimes think how differently I might have turned out if we had lived in separate houses. I might not even be the same person."

"Don't hold yourself in such low esteem," said Natasha fondly. "You're a good soul. I think you would have become yourself whatever adversities you had faced."

"Perhaps," said Kathryn. "Some people have no troubles, and they never learn compassion. Others suffer, and they choose to let it make them worse instead of better. Living with you has sharpened me. I don't know if I would have been ready— emotionally ready or spiritually ready—for this journey, if that had not happened."

Kathryn hugged her aunt and cousins a final time and boarded the train, unable to shake the feeling that she was being watched by reproving eyes. She was grateful at least that within a few minutes, she would be putting Boston behind her, this cold city of wharves, and churches with stone hearts. She had never felt entirely welcome here, and she had spent too much of her young life blaming herself for that. Only recently had she accepted that she had done nothing to provoke the mistreatment of others. She had simply existed, and apparently, that had been too much for some.

Ignoring the stares, she reached into her handbag and took out the trove of letters she had received over the past several months from her man out west. Late in January, she had come across an advertisement in one of the local dailies for a man who lived in Missouri seeking a Mail Order Bride. He owned a Hardware and Tinware Shop with his best friend and had been widowed after his wife died suddenly, shortly after giving birth to a pair of twins, a boy and a girl. He'd recently decided that he didn't want to continue trying to raise them alone. He was looking for a woman to be a wife and a mother to his twins.

Kathryn smiled as her eyes were drawn irresistibly to the paragraph where he had addressed her concerns about her physical appearance.

The color of your eyes don't bother me, he had written. *Mine are a muddy brown, like the Missisippi Mississippi after the spring floods. I never thought they were much to look at. I'd kill to have blue eyes, or even just one blue eye. I've never heard of anybody having two eyes of a different color before. I can't believe people have been giving you grief over it. I'd think they would find it enteresting. We get all sorts here in Rough Creek. You won't have to worry about nobody harassing you. I know a customer who got part of his arm torn off in a mining mishap. Another guy who lost a leg to frostbite during the great snowstorm. He ventured out into the snow for firewood and they found him a hours later, just ten yards from his front door, face down in the snow. Few more minutes and he'd have been dead. I reckon as long as you've got all your arms and legs—and even if you don't, maybe that'd be fine.*

Kathryn hugged the folded paper to herself like a treasured possession. The tone of the letter was so reassuring that she felt she loved the man without ever having met him. He didn't care what she looked like. Perhaps in time he might even come to find her beautiful. There had been no chance of anyone in Boston ever feeling that way about her. The men in Boston wanted a wife with fine features who knew her place and wouldn't bring disgrace to the family name. The one time she had nearly been involved with a boy, his mother had very quickly put an end to it. No one wanted their children or grandchildren potentially growing up with eyes of a different color. Over time, the burden of their fear had begun to weigh on Kathryn. She knew she was hated for no fault of her own. That didn't make it any better.

But Jacob loved her, Jacob wanted her, and that was more than enough.

CHAPTER 5

The journey west took three and a half days. The train pulled into the station just outside of Rough Creek at dusk on Saturday. Kathryn spent the last several hours of the journey sitting straight up in her seat, giddy and tense with anticipation, gazing through the window at the darkening prairies and the lush, verdant grass.

As the other passengers began to disembark, Kathryn smoothed her gown and hastily checked her appearance in a compact mirror, patting her hair down. Jacob would be waiting for her on the platform. By the end of the night—assuming he was true to his word and wasn't completely put off by her appearance—they would be seated together in his parlor or dining-room catching up on all the years they hadn't been together.

She wondered, with a sudden pang of apprehension, if she wasn't making a terrible mistake, but just as quickly put the idea out of her mind. Judging from their correspondence, they had a natural rapport. Something about them just felt right. No doubt that would remain true once they met in person.

Alighting onto the platform, it occurred to her for the first time that she had no way of knowing what Jacob looked like, apart from a few vague descriptions he had given in his first letter. She wondered if he would be able to discern the colors of her eyes in the half-darkness. If not, she would simply have to wait until the rest of her fellow passengers and the people they had been meeting cleared the platform. After a few minutes, an hour at most she thought, he would be the only one still waiting.

Kathryn seated herself on a bench facing the empty train, waiting for the crowd to thin out. Any time she saw a man standing by himself she half-wondered if maybe that was the man she had traveled all this way to meet. At one point, a young man even began to approach her, but then the woman he had been expecting called his name and he turned around with a start, greeting her with a look of relief and open arms.

She was attracting more attention here than she had wanted, already. Perhaps it was just her experience coloring her imagination, but she seemed to have drawn the disapproving stares of more than one gentleman. Whether because she was a lady seated by herself in an unfamiliar place or for the usual reasons, she didn't know. She wasn't sure she wanted to know. She wanted to go on believing, for at least a few minutes, that this was really the unprejudiced new home Jacob had promised her.

Nervously, Kathryn pulled the veil of her hat over her face. As the crowd began to trickle away and then vanish altogether, a new apprehension seized her. Supposing Jacob had stood her up? Perhaps he had changed his mind about wanting to marry her and had warned her not to come, in a letter that was still making its way to Boston via post. Perhaps he simply hadn't bothered to warn her at all. Or worse, maybe he had shown up to meet her on the train platform, taken a good look at her and melted away into the crowd. What would she do then?

With every couple that left the platform together, her worry intensified. Soon she was left completely alone in a darkness illuminated only by the light of a single overhanging lamp. It was perhaps the loneliest moment of her entire existence to that point. She had come all the way out here, and the man she had been intending to marry had reneged on his promise —had reneged and hadn't even warned her ahead of time.

She had been a fool to come all this way. She had been a fool to spend all that money—what had she been thinking? She should have waited and let the groom pay for it. She couldn't even afford the return trip home; she had spent it all on the trip west.

Panicking, worried that she was going to dissolve into tears here on the platform if she didn't do something, she settled on the one course of action that was still available to her. Jacob was known in town; he ran the only Hardware and Tinware Shop. It was likely that any random person she stopped in the street would know his name, would maybe even know where he lived. She'd find him one way or another. If he had changed his mind, she'd confront him about it. Perhaps, she could guilt him into paying her way back. At any rate, she wasn't going to leave Rough Creek before she found out exactly what had gone wrong and why he had stood her up. She wasn't going to spend the rest of her life wondering.

Leaving the station, she headed south toward the city lights along a well-trodden road that gradually widened. Lamps were lit in the upstairs rooms of some of the taverns, and in the windows, she could see men hunched over their desks writing, a man and woman having what looked like an argument, a child wistfully gazing down into the street. A carriage drawn by two black horses drove past her carrying two young couples facing each other and laughing. It was almost quaint compared to the bustle and hum of Boston, and yet there was something inexpressibly charming about it, like a village painting. Kathryn could almost imagine herself settling down in a place like this and raising a family. If only…

Around two corners and a few blocks down the city's main street, she found the general store, the interior of which was mostly empty of people at this time of night save for an older woman standing behind the counter beneath a decorative buggy whipcord that had been hung from the rafters. Reasoning to herself that if anyone in Rough Creek knew of Jacob and his whereabouts, it would be this woman, Kathryn strode up to her and said in a shy voice, "I'm sorry to impose… I've traveled out here looking for someone, and I was wondering if you could help me find him."

"Darling, I'm not a directory," the woman said slowly. "I can't tell you the name of everyone who lives in this town."

Kathryn was undaunted, however. "Then maybe you could tell me the location of his Hardware and Tinware Shop. You see, he manages the place."

The woman's face seemed to brighten a little. "Oh, if you're looking for Bailey, he works just a block down the street. He'll be closing up shop for the night. You might still be able to catch him, if you hurry."

"No, not Bailey," said Kathryn. "I'm looking for Jacob… Jacob Ashby. I'm guessing that's his partner."

"Oh, sweetie," said the woman, her face a mixture of concern and pity.

CHAPTER 6

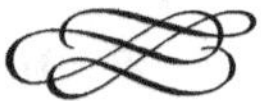

It was nearly closing time and Bailey stood alone behind the counter of his shop. The last customer had left an hour ago and since then, he had been searching for ways to distract himself so that he wouldn't have to think too hard about what had transpired here a few weeks before. Some nights were easier than others. He welcomed the arrival of customers because they were able to bring him, if only for a few minutes, out of the gloomy depths to which he was so prone.

When the door opened unexpectedly and a woman wearing a hat with a lace veil over it stepped into the room, he greeted her brightly with a deep sense of relief.

"Can I get you anything?" he asked. "You're lucky you showed up when you did; another ten minutes, and I'd have shut this place down."

"I'm looking for someone," said the woman, lifting her veil. Bailey was taken aback—both by her stunning appearance and the peculiar colors of her eyes. He had never known anyone to have one eye of a certain color and another eye of a different color. "I think he might work here with you."

Bailey shook his head, feeling suddenly timid in the presence of this woman's beauty. His throat felt dry and constricted. "Only person who works here is me," he managed to say. "Unless I'm the one you're looking for. Who sent you?"

The woman hesitated. "Is your name Jacob? Jacob Ashby?"

Bailey felt a twinge of pain and dread at the mention of the name. He wondered how long people were going to go on mistaking him for his partner. "No, I'm afraid not, ma'am. Jacob doesn't work here anymore." He studied the woman's face quietly. "Say, what brings you out here looking for him?"

He didn't know what he had been expecting her to say. Certainly nothing else could have equaled the shock of her next statement.

"We're to be married," she said. "We've been corresponding for the past three or four months. I traveled out here from the east coast with the intention of becoming his bride."

Bailey couldn't believe what he was hearing. Now he would have to give this woman the worst news of her life, and he didn't relish the prospect. A silence fell between them in which he struggled to form the appropriate words.

"I only just arrived in town tonight," the woman said.

"What's your name?"

"Kathryn." She smiled shyly. "My friends call me Kate."

"Am I the first person you've met in Rough Creek?"

She shook her head. "No, there was a woman at the general store, just now. Only I didn't get her name."

"What did she tell you?"

"I told her I was looking for a man named Jacob Ashby." Kathryn brushed her golden-blonde hair back. "Told her he'd invited me out here to marry him."

She seemed almost giddy now, as if the hardest part of her journey had ended, and her goal was in sight. It must have seemed like a dream long-deferred was now moments away from being fulfilled—as if Jacob were about to step out of a back room. Bailey cursed the fate that had made him the bearer of ill tidings.

"That would have been Beth Arden," he said aloud. "She owns the place. Sweet lady. What did she say to you when you told her?"

"She told me to come here," said Kathryn.

Bailey swore under his breath. Of course, she had. Beth wouldn't have wanted to be the one to break this poor young woman's heart.

He couldn't quite bring himself to look the woman in the face as he leaned over the counter.

"Kathryn, listen," he said slowly. "I don't know what to tell you. Jacob isn't here…"

"Here in the store, you mean?" she asked.

He shook his head. "Not here at all. In Rough Creek, or anywhere. He's dead."

Kathryn repeated the words back to herself, her gaze blank and perplexed. "But we've been writing… I only just got a letter from him a couple weeks back…"

"I'm sorry," said Bailey. "I really am. I know how hard this must be. And I wish you hadn't come all the way out here only for me to tell you this."

"When did he…?" She couldn't bring herself to form the word.

"Probably right after he sent you that last letter." Taking the damp cloth from the counter, Bailey mopped down his sweating face. "There was a robbery…"

"A robbery," she repeated, her eyes wide.

This was the worst he had felt since the day after the shooting, when the initial shock had started to wear away. The woman standing before him had plainly loved him, despite having not met him, and the vitality seemed to be draining from her face as she began to absorb the truth. She was already a different person from the innocent, bright-eyed woman who had come through the door just moments before. There was no bringing that woman back.

"I had stepped out for a few minutes," said Bailey. "If I'd been here, we might have been able to hold 'em off together. I think maybe they were waiting until I left, because they knew he would be outnumbered. If I hadn't gone across the street, he might still be alive."

"Who was waiting?" asked Kathryn. "I don't understand."

"There were bandits. I don't know if he told you, but this town has had a problem with bandits lately. The sheriff is at his wit's end. The murderers were never caught. They shot Jacob in cold blood and then leapt onto their horses and rode down the street, in view of all." Bailey had to grip the counter to steady himself. "I want them to be hanged. He was probably the best man I'd ever met."

Bailey realized too late that he probably shouldn't have said that; the sudden weight of his loss already lay heavy on the poor woman.

"B-but we were to be m-married," she said again. "We would have been so happy together... he had a couple of children, twins, and I-I was going to raise them… be a mother to them both…"

"Emily and Ethan," said Bailey. "They live with me now."

Kathryn glanced at him helplessly. "I hope you'll forgive me —maybe I ought to just let it go and return home, but I … I have to ask—would it be all right if I came home with you and saw them? Just once, before I go?"

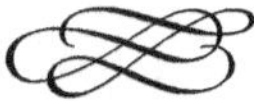

CHAPTER 7

An hour later, Kathryn was seated in a small room adjacent to the parlor with a single curtained window looking out on the windswept prairie. A piano stood in the room with a hymnal opened to a couple of Isaac Watts songs that she had grown up singing in her church choir. A small wooden chair with a cracked leg contained a large doll with blue button eyes wearing a gingham dress. The smell of roasting potatoes drifted in from the other room. There were a couple of other women in the house, one older and one younger. She could hear them chatting amiably as they made supper but couldn't make out what they were saying.

Kathryn didn't suppose it mattered much. This whole ordeal felt like a strange dream, like she had been inadvertently stranded on the moon or in another time and was trying to make her way home. Within a few weeks, assuming she could wrangle up the money to make the return journey, the people she had met here in Rough Creek would seem like half-forgotten figures out of an unhappy dream.

But for now, she was stuck in this dream world trying to ignore the sudden surges of grief that rolled up like waves from her chest. She was mourning the loss of a man she had never met. More than that, perhaps, she was mourning her dreams for the future. Jacob had been her one chance at a better life, and he was gone now. Soon she would be making her way back to Boston, where she felt so alone.

Lord, she found herself praying, *if there's any way out of this... Aunt Ruth isn't the richest person, and I don't know if she would be willing to shoulder this expense... but please, I don't want to be stuck here forever, not with Jacob gone.*

There was a tap at the door, and Bailey stuck his head in. "Supper's ready," he said. "You hungry?'

Kathryn nodded weakly. Food had been the last thing on her mind since she learned the news, but she didn't have any idea when she would get a chance to eat next. Rising from the chair, she followed him through the parlor and into the dining room where the younger woman was laying plates on the table while the two children—she knew from his letters that they were Ethan and Emily—fought with spoons.

"Hey, that's enough," said Bailey sternly. "You're gonna scoop each other's eyes out, and there's no doctor in the world that can put an eye back in once it's been scooped out."

"Eww!" cried Emily, setting down her spoon and covering her eyes with her small palms, but Ethan grinned wickedly.

"Dan Fennel," the older woman said, "told me a story about a hawk that flew down and took a little boy's eyes out and carried 'em away into the air. I bet he probably ate 'em!"

"Ma, Dan Fennel shouldn't be telling you stories like that. And neither should you," said Bailey. "Do you want the kids going to sleep having nightmares?"

"Well, you loved stories like that when you were a little boy," said his mother as she placed the potatoes and corn in the center of the table. "Children love to be scared, little boys especially."

"Once I asked old Dan why owls are so good at seeing in the dark," said Emily, "and he told me it's cuz they steal eyes from little girls. That's why I sleep on my face at night."

"Well, you're definitely not going over to see Dan anymore," said Bailey, plainly annoyed. "Anyway, we have a special guest tonight, and I want you both to be courteous and respectful." Motioning for Kathryn to take a seat next to him, he said, "Emily, Ethan, this is Kate. You can call her… what's your last name?"

It took her a moment to realize he was addressing her. "Oh, Sandridge."

"I want you to refer to her as 'Miss Sandridge,'" said Bailey.

"Did you say 'Miss' or 'Mrs.'?" asked Ethan. "Mrs. means you're married, don't it? Are you married? Don't you got a husband?"

"Ethan, that's impolite," said Bailey in a warning tone.

"What? I was only askin'." Taking up his spoon, Ethan began breaking his roasted potatoes down into chunks. "I was just wonderin' if you was married or not."

"You'll have to forgive the children," said the woman she now knew was Bailey's mother, seating herself at the head of the table. "They don't always know when to stop asking questions. I'm Faye, by the bye." She extended her hand across the table.

"The matriarch of the family," said Bailey. "She's the reason I'm not completely exhausted when my head hits the pillow at night."

"I get a lot of help from this one," said Faye, motioning to the younger woman, who had a mouth full of potatoes. "Elizabeth, say hello to the lady."

"Oh," cried Elizabeth, as if suddenly remembering her manners. She offered her hand, saw that there was a spoon in it, set the spoon down with a heavy thud and tried again. "Grandma gives me far too much credit. I mostly hover behind her in the kitchen and practice my dancing."

"Well, you're not wrong there," said Faye.

"Do you dance?" asked Kathryn.

"Not very well," said Elizabeth. "I'm better by myself. If there's a boy involved, I'll keep hitting him with my elbows or trying to go one way when he wants to go another way…"

"Sometimes she practices with a doll," said Ethan. "I seen her."

Elizabeth glared beadily at Ethan.

"Kate, I'm sorry you had to come all this way," said Faye, as she spooned a potato the size of a brick onto her plate. "Bailey has told me the circumstances of your coming out here, and I wish the journey had been more rewarding."

Kathryn nodded, not knowing what more there was to say. "Did you know him well?" she finally asked.

"I'd say so." Faye reached for the butter dish. "He was like another son to me. The twins practically live over here. And of course, they've taken up permanent residence ever since his passing."

"I gathered some lilies from the creek this morning," said Elizabeth, "and went down to the churchyard and laid them on his grave. I think I might go back tomorrow if you'd like to come with me."

Kathryn didn't want to go, but she sensed it was important that she did. "Yes, I would like that very much."

"And of course, you're welcome to stay here as long as you like," said Faye. "I've already spoken to Elizabeth about giving up her bed. She's agreed to sleep on a pallet on the floor for the duration. Unless you'd rather stay somewhere else."

"I'm afraid I don't have any money," said Kathryn, blushing slightly. "I couldn't afford a… a hotel for more than a night or two. I spent every penny I had making the trip out here. I should have been more patient, I see now. I should have waited to be sent a ticket. I know you'd probably prefer a lodger who could pay their way."

"Don't you worry about it," said Faye warmly. "You're welcome to stay here for as long as you need, whether that's a month or a year or more. That's what Jacob would have wanted."

"Did you know Jacob?" asked Ethan, surveying her with interest.

Kathryn nodded reluctantly. "We had spoken only through letters before. He wrote the most charming letters, full of hilarious asides about life in Rough Creek."

"Well, it's no picnic," said Faye, "though we do our best to make it livable. Admittedly, Jacob never mentioned that he had found a lady. I suspect maybe he was hoping to surprise us when he was suddenly married." She shook her head. "Poor soul, he must have been so excited."

For the first time, Kathryn was moved to wonder what he must have been thinking as he bled out on the sawdust-covered floor of that Hardware and Tinware Shop. Was he thinking solely of the twins? Or had his last thoughts been of her, and the life that they would no longer share, cut short by a bullet? The bandit who killed him had stolen decades from them.

"It won't be any trouble to me, sharing a room," Elizabeth was saying. "Grandma is always going on about how I need to make more friends my own age. And you're a little older, but not as old as Grandma."

"Perhaps you can take some lessons in decorum from a proper lady," said Faye. "Someone who doesn't fidget or break into song at odd moments or complain that her dress doesn't have nine tucks."

"Annie Applecart's dress has nine tucks," said Elizabeth, indignant. "You ought to see her walking down the street in that thing, she looks like the first breath of summer. Kathryn, did you bring any formal dresses?"

Kathryn was barely paying attention; she had just glimpsed Bailey watching her out of the corner of his eyes.

CHAPTER 8

A week passed. Kathryn had already written a letter to her aunt explaining Jacob's death and the fact that she was temporarily staying with the family of a close friend, but she hadn't yet worked up the courage to ask for money for the return trip—in part because in doing so she would be admitting that the trip had been a failure, and she should never have come; in part because she knew that Aunt Ruth didn't have the money, and there was no point in asking.

Still, she supposed there were worse things than being stuck with the Evans family in a settler community on the prairie. Faye was proving a particularly skilled cook—only the night before she had made parched corn, boiled ham, cornbread and fried potatoes, with pudding for dessert.

Despite their habit of arguing and asking questions incessantly, she found the twins charming. Ethan seemed mesmerized by her eye colors and kept asking her whether she had been born that way or whether she had stolen one of her eyes from a tramp on the trip from Boston. (Faye had scolded him for his impoliteness, but Kathryn took the questions in stride, calmly explaining that a falcon had dropped the eye from its long talons while she was out hunting). The truth was, Kathryn hadn't the foggiest idea why her eyes were colored the way they were.

Emily had sketched a portrait—shockingly good for a girl of five—in which Kathryn sat with her hands folded staring through a window, one eye conspicuously lighter than the other. Delighted by the portrayal, Kathryn had asked if she could keep it to take home with her, and Emily had said yes.

"I've never seen such talent in someone so young," Kathryn said to Faye one afternoon when the children were out playing with Elizabeth. "It's genuinely impressive. I hope she'll cultivate it and maybe pursue art as a career one day."

Faye was more cautious, however. Stirring the cider with a ladle, she shook her head sadly. "I've known many a talented person who never did anything with it. Better to be a good person, I think. Ain't much use for an art career out here. If I can get her to grow up decent, I'll feel like I've done my job."

"She's really good, though," said Kathryn emphatically. "Maybe I'm just easily impressed, but if you got her started early enough—if she took classes... Was Jacob an artist? I wonder if she got the skills from him."

Faye shook her head. "Jacob was talented in other ways, but it was Bailey, about a year or so ago, who got her interested in sketching. He was sitting in the parlor idly drawing a grasshopper sparrow from memory when she came over and asked what he was doing. He explained it and asked if she would like to try. Of course, she said yes, and found that she enjoyed doing it. I think at first, she was just trying to impress us—you know how children are—but over time, she's become quite a skilled little drawer."

Faye went on stirring the cider while Kathryn gazed through the window at the tall grass where the children's heads were just barely visible. Since coming to stay with him, she had been consistently impressed with Bailey's gentleness and patience toward the twins even when they were at their worst. Only once, when Ethan had been banging on a pan with a pewter spoon and wouldn't stop doing it despite being asked five or six times, had he lost his temper and dragged the boy to his room—for which not a single other person in the house blamed him, least of all Kathryn who was peculiarly susceptible to loud, sudden noises.

"And Bailey has never had children of his own," murmured Kathryn, not realizing that she had basically changed the subject. "I think he would be a good father."

"I suspect that he would," said Faye in a melancholy tone. "I'm not looking forward to the day when he'll have to give the twins up to a new family—if that should be necessary. I worry about him because he's gotten so attached. He's going to be completely heartbroken. But these children should have their own ma and pa. That's what we figured, anyway."

On the morning of her second Friday in Rough Creek, Kathryn was seated in the kitchen contemplatively drinking a glass of cold water when Faye came bustling into the room.

"I'm headed into town today," she said, "and I think I'll be taking the twins with me, so you don't have to watch them. I need to pick up some sewing notions, and we're almost out of potatoes because we've been going through so many. I think I might even buy some marmalade." She said this in a tone that made it sound as though marmalade was an unthinkable indulgence.

"Would you care if I came, too?" asked Kathryn. "Last night, I wrote a letter to my aunt, and I was thinking of heading down to the post office this afternoon to mail it. But if you're already headed that way, I'll just come with you."

"I don't mind if you come," said Faye, "as long as you don't mind the twins tagging along."

As if on cue, the twins came running together out of a back room, Ethan firing a toy gun in all directions while Emily ran heedlessly ahead of him carrying a stuffed cloth crow under one arm, her braid bobbing behind her.

"Emily, dear," said Faye gently, "you can't bring the crow to the store. People will give us weird looks, and I don't want them saying anything mean to you."

"Can't I, though?" said Emily miserably. "Corvus is a friend, and if anyone says anything nasty about him, he'll peck their eyes out!"

Faye laughed lightly. "Well, goodness, I don't want anyone to get their eyes pecked out, so I think it's best if you leave him here for now. It will be safer for everyone."

Kathryn smiled; she had been a somewhat morbid, spooky child herself growing up. Everyone had made fun of her for having demon eyes, so at some point, she had decided to lean into the rumors, terrifying her playmates with stories about ghostly women standing in windows and caterpillars the size of a man's head. By the time she had grown out of this phase, she did not have many friends left.

"Do you like birds?" she asked Emily as they walked through the front door into the blinding sunlight.

"Yes, I love them," said Emily cheerily. "Especially the big ones, the scary ones. I heard a story about a hawk that could rip a man's hair off!"

"I told you, he was wearing a wig," said Ethan matter-of-factly. "The hair came straight off because it weren't glued down properly."

"You don't glue your hair down," said Emily. "You nail it down."

They went on arguing all way to town, where Faye and the children parted ways with Kathryn just a block or two from the post office. The feeling of assurance and comfort that had followed her this far into town abandoned her the moment she and Faye separated. Kathryn hadn't realized until this moment how well they had succeeded in putting her at ease over the past few weeks.

Now as she crossed the street in the harsh light of midday, she felt the old certainty of being watched, of a hundred pairs of eyes on her waiting for her to trip over her own feet and vindicate their worst assumptions. As she handed her letter to the postmaster, he stared at her as if she had grown a third eye in the middle of her forehead, and no one at the house had wanted to tell her. He asked her a few questions in a terse voice about where she lived and what she was doing in Rough Creek. Kathryn answered in equally terse tones, feeling like she was being interrogated and wishing she hadn't left Faye.

"Where are you staying?" he asked, eyes still rooted to her face in a way that made her uneasy. "You got a family that can host you?"

"Please, I'd rather not talk about it," said Kathryn, feeling angry at herself even in the act of defending herself. The postmaster took the letter with a last baleful glare. With a surge of relief, Kathryn turned to the door, glad to be leaving the foul-smelling post office with the line of patrons who all seemed to be waiting impatiently, glowering at her as she left.

She didn't have any trouble finding her way down the street to the general store. It was the hottest part of the day, and a man stood leaning against a post outside the leather-tanner's, soaking his face with a wet cloth. A small, elongated hog knelt a few paces behind him, grubbing in the dirt for a green sprig that had grown up just under the porch. Both the man and the pig glanced up at her as she passed, as if her existence confused them. She couldn't help wondering how differently things might have been if Jacob had lived. She wouldn't have been some random woman, a stranger from out of town, but the wife of the Hardware and Tinware Shop's owner, and everyone would have had to respect her, if only grudgingly.

She reached the general store and was approaching the door when a man swung suddenly in front of her, blocking her path.

"Where are you headed, lady?" he asked quietly.

He was rakishly dressed in a patchwork checkered shirt, a pair of brown trousers and a wide-brimmed straw hat that seemed to be missing a chunk from one side. He was wearing no shoes. He sucked on a long piece of hay absently as he reached out a hand to grab a handful of Kathryn's hair.

"Never seen hair of that color before," he said in the same low voice. "Did you make a bargain with the devil for a head full of golden hair in exchange for those two devil eyes?"

Appalled by the man's advances, Kathryn swatted his hand back. At the same instant, however, a second man appeared behind her dressed just as shabbily as the first, wearing a red kerchief above his black eyes.

"Where you going, ma'am?" he asked in a voice of unnerving politeness. "I don't recall you even entering the store yet today. You leaving already?"

"Would be a shame to leave when you haven't even been inside," said the man in the straw hat. "A body would almost think you was trying to get away from us."

"But of course, she wouldn't be doin' that," said the man in the red kerchief. "Unless she really was some kind of witch…"

"I think she must be a witch," said the first, brazenly gesturing to her face. "That's the devil's mark. Them that are doomed to perdition are born with it."

"She ought to fit right at home here, then," said the second man, beginning to put his arms around her.

Kathryn let out a scream.

CHAPTER 9

Each day at around noon Bailey shut down the store for an hour or two, took a smoke break, and walked down the street to buy a meal at one of the local saloons. Prior to Jacob's death, the breaks had been only twenty minutes, a half-hour at most, but in the past couple weeks he had been delaying going back into work for as long as possible. If the family hadn't been depending on the income, he might have sold the store and found a different line of work. The strain of having to go in there day after day was beginning to wear on him.

Kathryn had proven a welcome distraction, though. Some people might have been repelled by her strange features, but he found himself wanting to sit down across from her at a table and stare silently into her eyes. Any time he caught her glancing at him for just a moment at dinner, his heart gave a sharp jolt. He would have given up any number of pleasures just to have her smiling at him every day the way he had seen her smile once or twice in unguarded moments.

It was foolish, he knew, to be nursing an attraction to someone who would likely be moving away forever in a week or two. And yet, he couldn't help it. He didn't know what he would have done if she had married Jacob. He would have had to pretend to be happy for them. Jacob had an uncanny way of reading him.

So did his mother, who had said to him the other evening, "Bailey, dearest, why don't you grab hold of that woman before somebody else does?"

It was easier to float through work now that he kept his thoughts preoccupied with Kathryn. With time and effort, he was learning not to think so much about the tragic events of a few weeks before. During the day as he minded the counter, he became absorbed in elaborate daydreams in which he and Kathryn took custody of the twins and raised them together in a house of their own. After a year or two, they would add a third child to the family, and then a fourth. Maybe eventually they would get a big dog. When Ethan got old enough, Bailey would take him grouse-hunting and teach him how to fire a real gun. Emily would go to Paris and become a famous artist and return a married woman with a family of her own.

Thoughts of this nature and a hundred more like them were circulating through his mind as he stood at the front of the store smoking his pipe—the pipe Jacob had left behind, which he had found on the floor of the store that day and painstakingly put back together. He returned the pipe to his pocket and was only just heading north in the direction of the Grey Turtle Saloon when he heard a scuffling in the street behind him, accompanied by a woman's shrill scream.

He knew who it was immediately. He knew, too, that it was the sort of scream a woman didn't make unless she felt herself to be in terrible and imminent danger. Turning abruptly around, he saw Kathryn standing near the front of Miss Erdman's store being accosted by two men in shabby clothes, both harboring a malevolent look in their eyes, from what he could see.

Bailey's stomach twisted into knots as he watched the man in the straw hat grab at her golden hair. They'd never discussed it openly, but he sensed how mindful she was of her appearance and how she dreaded going out in public for precisely this reason—because of the unwanted attention she drew. Without any further prompting, he turned and raced up the street, his feet pounding the dust, wanting to dig his hands into every inch of those hoodlums' flesh and tear it from the bones.

"LAY OFF OF HER!" he shouted savagely as he drew nearer. "Leave her alone! She don't want you—"

But the men only gaped at him, perplexed and a little amused. They looked the way a spider must look when a fly wanders willingly into its web.

"Well, lookie here," said Straw Hat, grabbing Kathryn by the arms and jerking her around. "Looks like somebody's taken a fancy to you."

"Couldn't imagine why," said Red Kerchief. "It's because you is a witch, maybe? Did you place a spell on the man?"

Kathryn kicked futilely back at their legs, looking mortified beyond measure.

Not feeling even a little intimidated by the fact that there were two of them and only one of him, Bailey strode forward and seized her from them, pulling her away. Kathryn leaned gratefully into him.

"If either of you imbeciles tries to lay a finger on her again," threatened Bailey, thrusting a hand into their faces, "you're gonna wish you had never stepped foot in Rough Creek."

Annoyingly, however, the two men only laughed. "You really think a small pint like you has the authority to drive us out of this town?" asked Straw Hat, spitting in the dirt at Bailey's feet. "Maybe you need to be given a lesson in who really runs things around here."

Red Kerchief looked him square in the eyes. "I'd be careful if I was you," he said. "I wouldn't want the Hardware and Tinware Shop to lose its *only* owner."

Something in the tone of his voice chilled the blood in Bailey's veins. The fool was taunting him with the memory of Jacob's death, using one tragedy to threaten another. Bailey stared hard into his face, trying his best to quell the rising tide of contempt and disgust. He couldn't place where, but he had seen those eyes somewhere before. Only once or twice in his life had he seen eyes of such hatred glaring out of a man's face, distorting his features.

"You don't frighten me," he said finally.

"Maybe not," said Straw Hat, now jovial. "But if you was a smarter man, you'd be scared."

"If one day you meet with an accident," said Red Kerchief, "it won't be our fault. We tried to warn you."

"Some people don't have a lick of brains in their heads," said Straw Hat. "Common sense would tell 'em to leave well enough alone, but they won't."

"Such do-gooders always come to a bad end," Red Kerchief added, shaking his head sadly. "It's a right shame, but it can't be helped none." He reached again for Kathryn's hair—she flinched and let out a whimper—but Bailey held up a warning hand.

"Well, there's no saving the fellow," said Straw Hat. "If he would just mind his own business and leave the lady to us… as the Good Book says, walk not after the way of fools or some such thing."

"Of course, he ain't gonna listen," said Red Kerchief. "These gallant idiots are always coming to bad ends over a woman. You'd think they would learn."

He made a nearly imperceptible motion with his right hand toward his holster—but just then the sheriff came rounding the corner on a black horse and turned in the direction of the general store.

"Keep an eye out for us," said Straw Hat with a placating smile. "I reckon this won't be the last time we run into each other."

"You'll find us hanging about," said Red Kerchief, casting a last lingering glance at Kathryn. "Around the store, outside your house, on the way to church…"

Bailey wanted to spit in their faces, but he wouldn't allow himself to stoop to their measure. He drew himself up to his full height, doing his best to ignore them, while he protected Kathryn behind him.

"You can't get rid of us," said Straw Hat, as he turned and began walking up the street, his partner following close at his heels. "Watch your back as you're closing up shop at night. You never know what might be creeping up out of the darkness."

"And on your way home," added Red Kerchief, though by now they were both some distance away. "If you were to get mangled to death on some rainy night, I don't know what could have done it."

"Not a clue," said Straw Hat, and together they turned the corner, laughing uproariously, and were gone.

Kathryn let out a deep breath, one that she seemed to have been holding in for several minutes and collapsed into Bailey's arms.

The sheriff rode up beside them. "Any trouble here?"

Bailey gave a snort. "Some fools is all. They're gone now."

The sheriff looked in the direction where the two men had disappeared. "Let me know if you see them in these parts again. Ruffians, the lot of them." He touched the edge of his hat and rode off.

Bailey stood stiffly, wanting to tighten his arms around Kathryn but not wanting to be too forward when she was already so badly frightened. He was conscious of her breathing, of the accelerated rate of her heartbeat, of her body pressed against his in ways that were both thrilling and uncomfortable.

"I'm so sorry they treated you like that," he said gently. "I won't let it happen again."

"I don't want you going and getting yourself hurt on my account," said Kathryn. "I think it's best if I leave Rough Creek."

Something in Bailey recoiled at the notion. He hadn't been prepared for the intensity of his gut response. "Look, not everyone here is like that. It's just them two men, those devils."

"And whoever killed Jacob Ashby," Kathryn replied.

"The majority of the folk in this town are decent, God-fearing men and women like my mother and Elizabeth," said Bailey, a little taken aback to hear her speak so candidly of Jacob's death. "They'd go to their graves defending you."

"Then why do I draw stares when I walk down the street? Why does a place fall silent the moment I enter?"

Bailey didn't have a good answer for this. Kathryn pulled away from him, fixing her mussed hair.

"Kate, don't think badly of us," he said. "I came running the moment I saw the way they was acting."

"And your defense is appreciated," said Kathryn curtly. "But I'd prefer to live where I can step out of my house without having to fear for my life—if there is such a place. I haven't found it yet."

"You think I don't fear for my life sometimes?" Bailey spoke sharply, heedless of the fact that people were beginning to pause in the streets. "You think I'm not aware that I'm risking my life every time I go into that store? But I do it because those children and my ma and my niece need to eat, and because… well, because I want to look after you."

"Well, you won't have to worry about me for much longer." Kathryn was hugging herself now, looking oddly cold and shrunken in the noonday sun. "I just sent a letter to my aunt in Boston. Maybe she can scrape together some money. Maybe the church will help me. I don't know. I just know I'm probably not going to be around for much longer."

There was something a little devastating, Bailey thought, in her calm acceptance of this fact.

"I know how one incident can turn you against a place," said Bailey, trying his best to mollify her. "I'd like to leave, too. If I didn't have family here—"

"Maybe you'll find you a pretty girl and head further west," said Kathryn in a cold tone. Then, seeing the injured look on his face, she added, "I'm sorry. I don't want you to think I'm ungrateful. They would've hurt me if you hadn't stepped in."

"No need to thank me," said Bailey gruffly, though his appreciation of her gratitude was plain on his face. "Why don't I walk you home now? I don't know where Faye and Elizabeth have gone to, but they was talking about making a red velvet cake for tonight's dinner. We'll have a real feast."

"A cake… I wish there was something to celebrate," said Kathryn, and, accepting his arm, she walked alongside him.

CHAPTER 10

Two nights later, Kathryn lay in bed with the twins on either side of her. She was reading a story from a collection of Hans Christian Andersen's fairytales, though she paraphrased slightly as she went along, and softened some of the more gruesome bits, so as not to confuse or frighten the children.

"It was New Year's Eve," she said, "and lights were shining out of every window as the little match-seller wandered the streets trying to keep warm. In the window of a shop, she saw a large roasted goose. Numb with hunger, she sank to her knees in the alley between two stores, her legs huddled together to keep out the cold that pressed at her hands and exposed face."

The two children listened soberly and quietly, with wide staring eyes, as the little match girl lit up all the matches in the vain hope of keeping herself warm. With each strike of a match she had a vision of families merrily feasting in their warm homes, followed by an apparition of her late grandmother who took her into her arms and led her to heaven. (Kathryn judiciously ended the story before the final scene, in which the little girl was found dead in the snow).

"Is that what heaven is like?" asked Ethan. "Will our ma come to get us before we die?"

"How will we recognize her?" asked Emily.

"You'll know her when you see her," said Kathryn.

"So if I see her standing over me, does that mean I'm about to die?" asked Ethan. "What if I look into a mirror and see her behind me?"

"You're not going to die yet." Kathryn smoothed the hair out of his face. "Not for a long time."

She and the twins and Bailey had spent most of the day together. Early that morning, as they ate their breakfast of johnnycakes, cornmeal mush and black, bitter coffee, Faye suggested to Bailey that he take the children into town for the annual late-spring festival.

"They've been getting a little restless lately," she said, "and it might do them good to walk around for a bit and burn all that excess energy."

Bailey asked Kathryn if she would like to join them.

"I know you might not want to go back into town," he said, "after the events of the other day. But I won't let nobody hurt you, promise."

To her own surprise Kathryn found herself eagerly consenting to go. Ever since the assault, she had found herself sitting closer to Bailey at breakfast and dinner and wanting to linger longer on the porch at sunset. She was surprised to realize that she felt safe with him in a way she rarely did with other men. It helped that he had been unusually attentive these past couple days, wanting to know how she was feeling and tending to her every comfort—bringing her pillows for her back, and brewing tea for her in the evenings as they sat outside and talked together, subduing the children when he could see they were badgering her.

Before, during her first week in the house, Bailey had been oddly aloof, and she assumed he was troubled by her strange appearance. As time went on, however, they were slowly beginning to warm toward each other, like a couple of house cats eyeing each other suspiciously and then curling up for a nap.

They left for the festival around noon. Kathryn was nervous at first—any time somebody brushed against her, she flinched in alarm, thinking the straw-hatted man had returned. But Bailey never left her side for an instant, and after an hour or two, she forgot her initial worries in the bustle of the crowds and the rows and rows of peonies and laburnums and delphiniums colorfully displayed. Bailey treated the twins to a bag of hard candy and then, to Kathryn's surprise, presented her a beautiful bouquet of spring flowers.

"Bailey, you didn't have to do this," said Kathryn. Somehow, the daffodils were rendered even more lovely by the fact that he had purchased them for her. "No one's ever bought me flowers before."

"I had a feeling that might be the case," said Bailey. "You're a woman who deserves to be given flowers, often. You'll likely be gone in a few weeks, and I won't be able to treat you like this."

The twins were hovering nearby as he said this, and Ethan brought up the exchange as they were lying together in bed that night.

"Where are you going?" he asked. "Are you dying?"

Kathryn couldn't help laughing. "No, I'm not planning to die yet. But I can't live here with you forever. One day, I have to go back to my own family."

"Why can't you just stay here and be a part of our family?" asked Emily. "That's what we're doin'."

Kathryn realized she didn't have a good answer to this question. "Because I-I don't belong with you," she said. "I have an aunt and cousins of my own."

"Do you have any children?" asked Emily.

"No, no children." Probably not ever, given the reaction of most men when they looked at her.

"Why can't we be your children?"

"Because…" she said slowly. "Because you already have Bailey and a grandmother to take care of you. And your auntie Elizabeth. I know they're not your birth father or birth grandmother, but they're raising you now, and they love you. They love you a great deal."

"What if we hid your things so you couldn't leave?" asked Ethan. "Would you have to stay here forever?"

"Where would you hide them?"

Ethan considered this question carefully for a minute. "In the fireplace," he said.

Kathryn laughed. "Then if all my things suddenly disappear, I'll simply go look in the fireplace."

"I tricked you," said Ethan. "They're hidden someplace else."

"I got an idea," said Emily in a tone of complete assurance that was striking in someone so young. "You and Bailey get married. Then you could be our ma and he could be our pa and we could all live together."

Kathryn felt as though the breath had just been knocked out of her. It was oddly similar to the startled feeling she had experienced the other day when the two men had approached her in the street. Now, fumbling for an answer, she glanced up at the door and was surprised to see Bailey standing there, quietly watching.

"I think that's enough questions for tonight," he said. "Kathryn is going to leave now so that you two can get some rest."

CHAPTER 11

Strange as it seemed, Bailey had been unable to stop thinking about Kathryn since the assault a few days earlier. The behavior of the two men had installed in him a fierce and mysterious urge to protect her. He found himself watching her more closely during meals, even when he didn't appear to be. Earlier that morning before they had left for the festival, Emily had come wandering out of her room with the most tragic look on her face and her arms caught in the sleeve of her shirt.

"Can you help me with this, Miss Kathryn?" she had asked sadly. "Sometimes, I'm bad at doin' things and Ethan makes fun of me."

Kathryn laughed as she beckoned Emily over and pulled her arm out of the sleeve, then adjusted and reinserted it.

"There you go, love," she said gently. "Now go and get your socks on so that you can be ready to go in a few minutes."

"All right," said Emily as she returned to her room, "but I still think it would be easier if you carried me the whole day."

Kathryn returned to her johnnycakes while Bailey gazed studiously through the window at the pearl-grey morning, wanting to preoccupy himself with anything but her.

"When I leave," she said, "I think I'll miss the two of them more than anything."

"You're much better with them than I am," said Bailey. "I get impatient sometimes, with Ethan especially, because he can be loud, and he jumps around a lot and he's at the age where he wants to contradict and question whatever I say."

"Boys are a handful," said Kathryn. "He'll grow out of it in time, though. Don't most of us grow up at some point?"

"Not all of us," said Bailey in a gloomy tone, and for a moment, they were likely both thinking of the wicked men they had encountered outside the general store two days before. His mother would have attributed their behavior to a bad upbringing, and maybe there was some truth to that. But he was troubled. After Jacob was killed, he'd thought to find a real family for the twins. One with a ma and a pa. But now, all he felt was confusion. The twins were getting settled in and he found that he was growing mighty fond of them. Could he give them up? Did he have to?

And now, here was Kathryn. He hadn't expected to be so strangely affected by the sight of her helping Emily with the shirt sleeve. It had moved him in ways he wasn't sure he entirely understood yet. Up until now, he had seen her as a lodger, as the fiancée of his late best friend and, more recently, as a woman who needed to be loved and protected… but no more than that.

Now, for the first time, it occurred to him what an excellent spouse she would make for someone, provided they weren't bothered by her unusual eyes—which hadn't bothered him as much as it seemed to bother others. He wasn't naïve; he had seen the glances people gave them as they walked up the street, even if she hadn't. The more he got to know her, the more it irritated him. No one was less deserving of scorn and vitriol than Kathryn. She deserved to live in a fine house and to be given every comfort that a man could afford to give her.

There was something about Jacob's death that had been bothering him for weeks, though he had managed to brush it aside during the initial shock of his loss. Now though, with Kathryn becoming an immovable force in his life, he found himself puzzling again over those final words Jacob had spoken as he lay bleeding out behind the counter.

"Promise that you'll take care of the twins for me," he had said. "That you'll make sure they're fed and clothed and properly educated. A new mother… C-can you do that?"

Of course, Bailey had promised that he would, without really being sure what he was agreeing to. Now for the first time, he began to wonder if maybe there had been a secret meaning implicit in those final words. Maybe Jacob had meant that he wanted Bailey to marry Kathryn and for them to raise the children together, since he could no longer do it. Maybe he had been giving his blessing to their union.

It was possible he was reading too much into the words, of course. *Promise that you'll take care of the twins for me.* Maybe he had simply meant that he wanted Bailey to find them a set of new parents. Maybe Bailey was being presumptuous in trying to guess what might have been going on in the brain of a dying man. But the fact remained, Kathryn had already been on her way to Rough Creek, and Jacob had been planning to marry her when she arrived. He had already selected her as their mother. Would he be disrespecting Jacob's wishes, now, if he left them in the hands of someone else? If anyone other than Kathryn were to become their mother?

After Kathryn had finished putting the children to bed, Bailey returned to his own room where he spent an hour reading by lamplight. At around ten, he emerged to find Kathryn seated on the love seat in the parlor silently working on a half-finished embroidery. Bailey sat down next to her and for a few minutes, they sat together in a silence that was only broken by Elizabeth singing loudly and slightly off-key in another room.

"The hardest part of a project like this is the half-way point," said Kathryn, when no one had spoken in a great while. "Once you're past that, the second half goes fairly quickly."

"How long do you think it will take you to finish?" asked Bailey.

"No more than a couple days." Kathryn smiled, as if pleased that he was showing an interest in her work. "Depending on whether I can find the energy to work at night once the children have gone to bed. Like tonight. Corralling them takes so much out of a person."

"I hope it hasn't been too much," said Bailey. "I know Ethan could drive a man to hard liquor."

"He's a sweet boy, though," said Kathryn. "I think that someday he'll be a boon to the community. And Emily has such a lively imagination—the other day she was trying to tell me that she had been born from an egg that came out of a fish's mouth and bobbed on the water for several weeks before she struck land." Kathryn shook her head. "Honestly, how does she think of these things?"

"It probably helps that you've been reading her fairytales," said Bailey. He was having to resist a mysterious impulse to put his arm around her. "My mother insisted on reading to us every night growing up. She said a man couldn't grow up properly unless he was read to."

"Maybe that's what was wrong with those men we met the other day," said Kathryn, shifting uneasily in her seat. "Nobody read to them when they were boys. Nobody taught them to love reading."

"Well, we're not going to make the same mistake with this boy," said Bailey, yawning. It would have been the perfect moment to stretch and place an arm behind her, but somehow, he held himself in check. "I can't control what happens to them once they leave this house, but as long as they live under this roof, there will be books a-plenty."

Kathryn beamed, taking an evident pleasure in his care for the two children. "I love that you're committed to their welfare," she said, "even though they don't truly belong to you."

"I have to be," said Bailey. "It's what Jacob would have wanted."

Silence fell between them. Bailey wondered whether he had said the wrong thing by invoking Jacob's name. He didn't want to be insensitive when he knew how much she had liked him. They rarely talked about him, and Bailey assumed she hadn't brought him up because the grief was still too fresh.

"I'm sorry—"

"Don't be," said Kathryn abruptly. "You haven't done anything wrong. I can't imagine Jacob wanting them to be raised by anyone other than you."

"The longer they stay here, the harder it's going to be for me to let go," replied Bailey. "If a new family surfaces, they may have to be pried out of my arms."

"I feel the same," said Kathryn. She blushed faintly, as if not wanting to admit how attached she had grown to them. "The best part of every day is getting to lie there in bed between the two of them at night. I love the questions they ask, and their little faces of surprise as I read to them from Andersen's fairytale book. I almost wish I could take them home with me."

"You've taken exceptionally good care of them," said Bailey in a tone of fierce tenderness. "I wish you didn't have to go. I wish I was capable of being everything they need. Once you're gone, the silence is going to be awful. I'll be begging Elizabeth to sing something just to drown out the hum of your absence."

"Maybe they don't have to leave," said Kathryn. "Wouldn't you love to be the one to raise them?"

"Wouldn't you?" Bailey replied.

No one said anything for a moment. Bailey could practically feel the tension coursing between them like an electric current. Then, seized by a sudden impulse, he reached over and ran a hand along her cheek. Kathryn caught her breath but didn't flinch.

"I wish people weren't always going places where I can't go." Feeling emboldened, he continued to caress her cheek. "Jacob is dead, my elder sister is dead, these children I love as if they were my own might not always be with me. I've no idea what the future might hold. And as far as you—"

He couldn't bring himself to say it—couldn't bring himself to acknowledge that soon she would be returning to a place where she would be as good as dead to him. Transfixed by her eyes, he said quietly, "Has anyone ever told you how incredibly beautiful you are?"

He could tell by the look on her face that no one had. A tear formed in the corner of one eye.

"A woman doesn't get a lot of compliments," she managed to say, "when she looks the way I look."

"I reckon that doesn't say much for the intelligence of most people," said Bailey, his heart thrumming rapidly. "I was gripped from the second you walked into my store. Beauty like that, you only see in paintings or museum statues. I never expected to see anything like it in the flesh."

"You give me far too much credit," said Kathryn, abashed but not upset.

"No, not enough," said Bailey, "not nearly enough," and, not being able to contain himself any longer, he leaned forward and kissed her fervently upon the lips. Kathryn didn't resist; in fact, he was surprised to find her kissing him in return. He wanted to freeze their position in that moment forever—before she got up and went to bed for the night and then packed up her belongings and left the house. He wanted to hold her so close to his heart that she couldn't go. He wanted to go on kissing her until the grass grew under their feet.

CHAPTER 12

It was a week later, on a sleepy Friday afternoon. In an effort to keep himself awake, Bailey sat behind the counter at the store ruminating on the memory of the kiss he had shared with Kathryn. He was alone in the store save for two customers who were murmuring quietly to one another as they browsed the shelves in the back.

"It's been a while since I've eaten goose," said the woman, whose name was Marguerite. "I'd give my right arm to go home tonight and have an enormous, fat goose, fully cooked, dressed and waiting for us on the dining-room table."

"Hard to find a good goose around here," said her husband, a taciturn older gentleman named Henry.

Bailey gazed through the outside door onto the crowded street. Kathryn and Faye had gone to the general store but promised to stop in on their way back to the house. He and Kathryn still hadn't discussed the conversation they'd had on the love seat the week before. They hadn't spoken much at all, in fact. Kathryn had been oddly shy and often retired to bed as soon as the twins fell asleep.

Bailey was beginning to worry that perhaps she resented him for transgressing some unspoken boundary. He ought to have at least explained what he had been feeling before surprising her with a kiss. Now the tension that hovered between them like a squat owl was likely going to accelerate her departure from the house. In his braver moments, he wondered if he ought to address his attraction before she left Rough Creek forever. He knew he'd regret it if he waited; and he also knew she was never going to bring it up on her own. Bailey didn't want to bring it up, but he reminded himself that he wasn't confronting her just for his own sake, but for the sake of the children, who needed a mother.

As soon as the thought crossed his mind, though, he could almost hear Kathryn saying, "Is that all I am to you? Just someone to raise the twins?"

And of course, the answer to that was no, she was so much more… his willingness to embarrass himself the other night ought to have proven that once for all. You didn't kiss a woman like that unless you truly cared for her.

"I don't know if you heard," Marguerite was saying, "but Florence Rigbee was down at the sheriff's office the other day, and she heard the sheriff saying that he thinks those bandits are still holed up in town."

"What, you mean the ones who killed…?" He lowered his voice, as if fearing that Bailey might overhear. "If they was smart, they would have turned tail and skipped town after shooting that poor man in cold blood. Why hang around here where they're likely to be caught and hanged?"

"That's what's keeping the sheriff up at night," said Marguerite. "He says it's because the bandits aren't afraid of him. If there was a shootout, they figure they would have the upper hand."

Henry clearly shivered, though likely not from cold. "Almost makes you afraid to leave the house," he said. "We had better hurry home. It's getting late…"

"Yes, and I'm making a roast tonight," Marguerite said as they left the store. "It's going to take a couple hours at least to peel and boil them potatoes and get the meat…"

Bailey watched them go, wishing they hadn't left him alone in the now-empty store. He hated to think of the bandits strutting through the middle of town with impunity, convinced they could kill anyone they wanted and get away with it. They were so sure they would suffer no consequences for having murdered Jacob, and the sad truth was, they were probably right. In his darker fantasies, the ones Bailey only indulged in as he was falling asleep at night, he imagined himself purchasing a pistol and gunning them down in the street. But of course, that was a foolish idea… It was cowardly to shoot a man when his back was turned, and if they saw him approaching, he would be dead before he got within ten paces.

There were moments, too, when he wondered if Kathryn quietly resented him for having lived when her own fiancé had died. Maybe she wished that Bailey had died in his stead and that Jacob had survived to marry her and run the store. Part of him wished that, too. It would have made more sense, given that Jacob already had a family and Bailey had no one and nothing.

Killing a father on the eve of his wedding week and allowing a man with no spouse or children to go on living seemed like a senseless waste on the part of the universe. It didn't square with his understanding of how things were supposed to work. No, it would have made much more sense for him to die, if anyone. He would never have met Kathryn, of course, but maybe she would have been better off. She would rather have married Jacob than him, anyway.

Undoubtedly the twins would have been happier, too. All week, he had been thinking about the question Emily had asked Kathryn on the night of the kiss, the one that had left her speechless.

"Are you and Bailey going to get married? Would you be our new ma and pa?"

In a way, he was glad she had asked the question, because at least it had forced Kathryn, if only for a moment, to consider the issue. He'd love to have heard her response. He was sure now that they wouldn't find a better mother than Kathryn, though he wondered if he was quite up to the challenge of being their pa. Could he ever make her happy in the way that Jacob surely could have?

He shook his head. Foolish, useless thoughts, he scolded himself.

Kathryn had left Faye in the general store sleepily examining fabrics while she nipped out to the post office. This time, no one hassled her and even the postmaster's eyes didn't linger long on her face as he handed her a letter from Boston. Overjoyed to see that her aunt had written, Kathryn placed the letter in her brown leather satchel and turned to leave.

She strode up the street past the Hardware and Tinware Shop and the milliner's and the leather-supplier's. It was the hottest part of the day and perspiration lay thick on the back of her neck, running down and soaking her bodice. She was looking forward to getting back inside and finding some place cool and quiet where she could read her letter.

Entering the general store, she spotted Faye standing near the back by herself and was making her way toward her when a shadow darkened the doorway and a shot rang out.

Several people screamed. Kathryn froze in mid-stride and turned around, seeing the frightened faces of the women standing behind the counter and painfully conscious of the fact that Jacob had died in precisely this way.

There in the doorway stood the two men who had harassed her on the porch the week before, eyeing the patrons with looks of cold malice. The man in the straw hat took an orange from the top of a barrel and bit into it without even bothering to remove the peel. He didn't seem perturbed by the presence of the peel; indeed, he hardly seemed to notice.

"So as you've probably guessed," he said, "this is a hold-up. Don't try to resist, and we might let you live, maybe."

"The name is Joe, and this here is Leo," said the man in the red kerchief, "and we'll be taking your things. Lay down flat on your stomachs so I don't have to do anything I'm going to regret later. Blood is such an awful thing to clean up, ain't it?"

"Never comes out, no matter how hard you scrub the wood," said Leo sadly. "If I have to shoot even one person, I might just lose my temper, and you don't want me to lose my temper."

Thinking it was best not to draw their attention, Kathryn sank to her knees on the floor behind a barrel full of vinegar, her eyes peering over the rim just enough that she could see the two men as they approached Faye, whose face had gone bone-white as she slowly lowered herself to the ground. At the front of the store, Beth Arden was very conspicuously reaching for the gun she kept under the counter. Leo, who had obviously witnessed this scene play itself out several times before, nonchalantly walked back behind the counter and snatched it from her.

"Thank you, ma'am," he said with a faux-gallant air. "Would be a terrible shame if you tried to use this thing. Wouldn't want you to end up like the poor fool up the street who thought he could take on me and my brother."

Kathryn let out an audible gasp. Leo's head swiveled like an owl beneath his hat, and he turned to look at her with wide, probing, excited eyes.

Kathryn could see at once she had made an awful mistake. The two men now seemed to have forgotten their original purpose entirely as they strode rapidly across the store toward her.

Several things then happened at once.

First, a third man came walking into the room. He had a grizzled face lightly shadowed by a goatee and wore a red flannel shirt with dark trousers torn at the knees. They were torn in perfect symmetrical lines, as if he had done the tearing himself. Stooping to pick up part of the rind that Leo had flung onto the floor, he crammed it into his mouth and began knocking over tables and displays, which elicited screams from the prostrate figures, mostly women, who lay on the floor.

At almost the same instant, Leo came running over and, grabbing Kathryn by the collar of her dress, forcibly pulled her into an upright sitting position as if he were lifting a cat by the neck. Kathryn's heart raced furiously as she felt cold steel pressing against her skin.

"What larks," he said with a sardonic laugh. "What a weird happenin' that I should find you here without that handsome oaf to protect you. The Lord truly works in mysterious ways."

Kathryn wanted to reply that Bailey was working a mere block away, but remembering the fate of her fiancé, she dared not. When she opened her mouth to retort, the words wouldn't come. Her tongue felt dry and heavy.

"Here's what we're gonna do, princess," said Leo low in her ear. "It's only a matter of minutes until the sheriff gets here, and I'd like to be gone before he does. The rest of this crew can stay here and rot, but you're gonna come with us. And I don't want to hear a word of complaint, ya hear?"

Kathryn nodded miserably. Even in the unlikely chance she made it to the end of the day alive, they would be far from town by sundown and she knew, with a horrible twisted feeling in her belly, that she would be better off dead.

But at present, there was no point in resisting. As long as Leo held the gun, she would have to do whatever he wanted. Wrapping a hand tightly around her wrist, he jammed the pistol into the small of her back.

"We're going to walk toward the door now," he said, "and I don't want you to scream or open your mouth."

Kathryn nodded to signal that she had understood. A tight lump had formed in her throat as thoughts of the twins flashed across her mind unbidden. Prodding her forward with the pistol, Leo led her outside into the glaring and oppressive sunlight where his two comrades were already waiting.

"Why don't you two go on ahead," he said with an ominous smile. "I'll catch up later. Right now, I've got me some business to attend to with this gal."

CHAPTER 13

Bailey knew something was wrong because the streets had fallen silent.

This had happened once before, in the moments before Jacob's death—traffic on the main street had come to a standstill, the town seemed to be holding its breath… and then the running had started, and the yelling. Now as he came out from behind the counter and gazed through the door onto the street in front of the store, everyone seemed to be turned in the direction of the general store, waiting. Bailey hailed down a child of ten dressed in a grey flat cap.

"What's going on in there?" he asked.

"Two bandits entered the store not ten minutes ago," said the boy, "followed by a third. You couldn't pay me to go in there."

"Why don't you run and get the sheriff?" asked Bailey, perplexed by the helplessness of the bystanders. Shoving the boy lightly to get him moving, Bailey began walking against the crowd in the direction of the store, knowing full well that Kathryn and Faye had been planning to visit the store that afternoon. He hadn't gone more than a few paces, however, before his worst fears were confirmed: the door swung open and two of the bandits emerged, followed by a woman with a gun to her back.

Even from a distance of fifty paces, Bailey could see everything clearly. His heart was beating hard enough to rattle his frame as he studied the shadowed face beneath the straw hat and realized where he had seen those cold, laughing eyes before—emerging from his own store on the day of Jacob's death.

Bailey waited until the other two bandits had taken to their horses and fled the scene, then, with a fearlessness he hadn't known he possessed, he began running up the street in the direction of the bandit and Kathryn. Never mind that the bandit was armed, and he wasn't; he would have been an unforgivable coward if he let the man drag her away without a proper fight.

Seeing him approaching, Leo spat on the ground at Kathryn's feet, looking more amused than frightened.

"About time you done showed up," he said. "I was starting to worry this was gonna be too easy."

Bailey didn't dignify the comment with a response. His blood was on fire; hot malice animated his limbs as he blazed forward, wanting to rip the beating heart from the man's chest and stomp on his entrails. Leo, taken slightly off-guard by the swiftness and intensity of his approach, didn't think of changing the direction of his pistol until Bailey was only about ten yards away. He let go his grip on Kathryn and prepared to shift, but it was too late—Bailey was already on top of him like a nest of hornets.

Kathryn let out a low exclamation of horror as the two men scuffled in the dirt, digging their nails into each other's arms, pummeling whatever soft bits of flesh they could reach. Leo slammed his head into Bailey's chest, winding him; Bailey retaliated by planting a knee in his belly.

The crowd was scattering, composed of people who were slowly emerging from the store and running away. Those who had been in the street when the bandits attacked took cover, but Bailey was largely heedless of their attentions as he grabbed at Leo's face and pulled his hair back. Leo gave a low, dog-like snarl and bit him on the neck just enough to draw blood. Enraged, Bailey attempted to knee him in the groin but missed. Leo gave a savage smile of triumph as he grabbed for his pistol and brought it down hard on the top of Bailey's head.

Leo's repeated blows and jabs were beginning to have an effect. Bailey was losing blood, losing the ability to think properly. The world seemed to be darkening around him, the voices growing fainter and fainter…

"On the bright side," growled Leo, "you'll be seeing your friend soon. Say hello to him for me."

Bailey felt a swelter of rage in his gut that might have fueled a dozen blows if he hadn't already been so faint from loss of blood. He was close to passing out, or worse, and he didn't know how much longer he could hold on. Kathryn stood over them, her features barely discernible, silhouetted against the storefront, hands over her face. She took a long look at Leo lying there, snarling and spitting… and then, with one solid, well-timed kick, she sent him rolling over into the reddish dirt, clutching his sides in agony and calling her filthy names that made Bailey want to drive a stake through his eyes.

But now that Leo had, for the moment, relinquished his grip, Bailey felt a resurgence of strength. Raising himself to an upright position, he reached over the injured bandit's chest and groped for the pistol that he had dropped at his side in the eddying dust. With the last ounce of his strength, Bailey aimed the pistol carefully, resisting the overwhelming impulse to murder him outright, and shot him once in the lower leg.

Leo let out a satisfying yelp of pain, like a dog in its death throes, as blood pooled from the wound in his leg. At almost the same instant, the sheriff on horseback rounded the corner in front of the Hardware and Tinware Shop and came trotting up to the spot where the men lay.

"Well, it looks as though you managed to subdue this low-life with no help from me," said the sheriff with a glow of satisfaction. "This scum's two compadres were just apprehended cutting a path out of town. With your help, we've managed to capture all of them in one day."

Kathryn put an arm around Bailey's waist and helped him to his feet. Somehow the feel of her body pressed against his overwhelmed the satisfaction of having bested the killers. "You hear that, Kate?" he said with a forgivably smug smile. "Looks like you might be able to walk about in this town after all."

"I'm not planning on going anywhere," said Kathryn, and gave him a lingering kiss on the cheek.

Kathryn and Bailey were married a month later, on a warm summer day.

Aunt Ruth and the cousins were able to come for the wedding, Ruth having acquired an adequate undisclosed sum from her father, who had just died after a prolonged illness. She sat alongside the twins, keeping a tight grip on the exuberant Ethan, as their new parents were wed in a brief outdoor ceremony in a garden fragrant with buttercups, hydrangeas and lilies of the valley.

After the exchange of vows—after they shared their second kiss—the guests enjoyed a small reception featuring ham, roasted chicken, and strawberry, peach and rhubarb pies hand-made by Faye and Elizabeth, both who had hardly slept in the days leading up to the wedding.

During the reception, Aunt Ruth came up and offered the groom a kiss on both cheeks. "When she wrote to tell me that Jacob had died, and that she was coming home, I prayed she might find a husband here in Rough Creek. I'd have been right disappointed if she had returned a single woman."

"I didn't want to let her go," said Bailey with a chuckle. "The longer she stayed, the more I was tempted to tie her to a chair in the kitchen."

"I wouldn't have complained much if you had," said Kathryn, looking particularly radiant in her white lace gown and her hat with the veil on it. Then, she laughed.

Later that night, after the twins had gone to bed, she and Bailey sat together on the front porch. Kathryn stroked his arm lovingly as he smoked his pipe, staring up at the night sky in a dreamy sort of way.

"How many planets do you think there are up there?" he asked after a long but relaxed silence. "And out of all those planets, how many married couples who are really happy?"

"Not more than a hundred, surely," said Kathryn. "How many married couples have you known here who were really happy?" Her eyes gleamed cat-like in the half-light as she turned to him and added, "Do you think we'll be happy together, always?"

"I can't imagine being this happy without you in my life," said Bailey, placing an arm on her shoulders.

"Yes, but we were only just married this afternoon. Suppose troubles come?"

"I'm sure they will." He took a philosophic puff on his pipe. "But when they do, I'll remind myself how much worse they could have been. We might have never been married, and the twins might have gone to live with someone else. It was a benevolent providence that brought you all this way from Boston."

Kathryn rested her chin on her hand. The thought of them never having met was almost too terrible to contemplate.

"I'm going to wake up every morning and remind myself of my good fortune," she said. "That way I'll never be cross with you, and never take you for granted."

"You're welcome to be cross with me," said Bailey, "but I'll still love you, regardless."

"Maybe this is why couples fight and are unhappy," said Kathryn quietly. "Because they've never considered their good fortune. How lucky, how truly lucky we are to have each other."

Bailey stooped and planted a single kiss on the top of her head. "And to think that you were wearing a veil on the night we first met. I was almost deprived of seeing your best feature."

Kathryn laughed lightly. "I suppose I should have known we belonged together when you wouldn't stop looking into my eyes."

"Has no one else looked into them before?"

"They have, but not with love." Kathryn stroked his leg fondly. "Not with your unabashed delight and devotion."

Bailey smiled. "I hope to see those eyes every morning when I wake. And I hope to fall asleep after looking into them every night."

"If I didn't know any better," said Kathryn lightly, "I'd think it was my eyes you had fallen in love with, instead of me."

"Imagine how different you'd be without them," said Bailey. "Your sweetness… your sympathy for the less fortunate. You might have gotten married in Boston and never been drawn out here to Rough Creek."

"And would that have been the worst thing?"

Bailey kissed her again, grazing her ears with his lips. "Yes. It would have been." He motioned up at the velvety sky. "On one of those planets there's bound to be some poor fool just like me, trying to raise a pair of twins on his own… only he never met a Kate. I feel sorry for him."

"Probably his Kate exists somewhere, he's just never met her."

"Maybe he never will," said Bailey. "Wouldn't that be tragic?"

"We should pray for them to find each other. Can you pray for people on other planets?"

"I don't see why not." Bailey took a last drag of his pipe and returned it to his shirt pocket. "Maybe somebody somewhere was praying for us. Maybe that's how we met. These sorts of things don't happen just by chance."

"I wish I knew who it was so I could thank them," said Kathryn. "And let them know that they, and you, have made me the happiest of women."

"And me, the happiest of men," said Bailey.

Kathryn rose slightly and Bailey tilted her chin up, giving her a lingering kiss on the lips. "Promise me you'll never forget what an extraordinary set of circumstances it took to bring us together."

"Never, never," said Kathryn. And they went on kissing while the wind stirred the grass and brushed against the windows, as though in celebration.

The End

CONTINUE READING...

Thank you for reading *A New Mother for the Twins!* **Are you wondering what to read next?** Why not read *Fighting for His Bride?* **Here's a peek for you:**

Riding his blue roan across the foothills of the Rockies, Jonesy reined in for a moment to admire the view. Hooking his left leg around the saddle horn, he watched a pair of hunting hawks far below him. They soared over the lower hills that fed into the plains before vanishing from his sight.

"Hawks mate for life," he mused aloud. "Maybe they know something I don't."

Jonesy tried not to ponder his solitary existence too often. When he did, in moments like this one, he got to thinking of a long life ahead of him with no one to share it with. That led to thoughts of never having a son to follow him, or a daughter to see grow up and marry. Then those imaginings lead to depression and loneliness that he would find difficult to shake.

"All right, time's a wasting," he commented to Doncaster. "No time for wishing things was different. We got cows to check."

The roan gelding's ears flicked briefly back toward Jonesy before swerving forward when something caught his attention. Jonesy put his boot back in his stirrup, and clicked his tongue, moving Doncaster into a quiet walk further up the hill. Before his loneliness dug in deep, he pondered finding a wife.

"Now what sensible gal would wanna set up housekeeping with an ugly ole cowboy like me?" he asked his horse. Not receiving much of an answer, Jonesy went on. "I mean, look here, it's not like there are plenty of gals in the town of Shallow Gorge, you know. Pert near every gal is married, and those that ain't are widows old enough to be my mama. You see the problem here?"

Doncaster didn't answer, but his ears and attention remained fixed on something ahead of them. Jonesy tried to see what he either saw, smelled or heard, but only a line of pine, evergreen, and scrub oak stood ahead of them. He started to speak again but thought better of it. Though he enjoyed his conversations with his horse, sometimes he had to listen to what Doncaster might be telling him.

Choosing to ride around the thicket rather than follow the trail through it, Jonesy suspected Doncaster might be onto something when his head rose to see better. Then he heard a horse snort from behind the next line of trees, and Jonesy suddenly knew what his gelding had been telling him all along.

Kicking Doncaster into a lope, Jonesy also reached for the Winchester rifle in its scabbard. Clearing the trees, he saw the two men crouched over the carcass of one of his cows, their skinny mounts standing nearby.

Visit HERE To Read More!

http://ticahousepublishing.com/mail-order-brides.html

THANKS FOR READING!

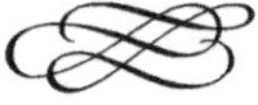

If you **love Mail Order Bride Romance, <u>Visit Here</u>**

https://wesrom.subscribemenow.com/

to find out about all **<u>New Susannah Calloway Romance Releases!</u> We will let you know as soon as they become available!**

If you enjoyed *A New Mother for the Twins,* would you kindly take a couple minutes to leave a positive review on Amazon? It only takes a moment, and positive reviews truly make a difference. Thank you so much! I appreciate it!

Turn the page to discover more Mail Order Bride Romances just for you!

ABOUT THE AUTHOR

Susannah has always been intrigued with the Western movement - prairie days, mail-order brides, the gold rush, frontier life! As a writer, she's excited to combine her love of story with her love of all that is Western. Presently, Susannah lives in Wyoming with her hubby and their three amazing children.

www.ticahousepublishing.com
contact@ticahousepublishing.com